Piggity Wiggity Jiggity Jig

by Diana Neild
Illustrated by Philip Webb

SCHOLASTIC

For David, Susannah, Michael and Sylvia ~ DN

For Thomas, Katherine and Benjamin ~ PW

First published in 2008 by Scholastic New Zealand Limited
This edition first published in 2011 by Scholastic Children's Books
Euston House, 24 Eversholt Street
London NW1 1DB
a division of Scholastic Ltd
www.scholastic.co.uk

London ~ New York ~ Toronto ~ Sydney ~ Auckland
Mexico City ~ New Delhi ~ Hong Kong

Text copyright © 2008 Diana Neild
Illustrations copyright © 2008 Philip Webb

ISBN 978 1407 11584 9

1 3 5 7 9 10 8 6 4 2

Piggity-Wiggity Jiggity Jig
was a long sort of name for a short kind of pig.

His dad was a chef at a city café;
he made croissants and quiches and soup-of-the-day.

His mum very proudly looked after their nine
and would finish the day with a small glass of wine.

The home of the Jigs, with its welcoming air,
had been built in the thirties, constructed with care.
A muddlesome, cuddlesome, comfortable place,
with a surplus of playthings and marginal space.

There were muffins,
and milk warmed in muggity-mugs,
tempers and tantrums and huggity-hugs.

But at bedtime one night, having stories with Dad,
Piggity-Wiggity felt a bit sad.
He knew that it couldn't be terribly wrong,
but nobody else had a name that was long.

His family had names that were commonly used,
but his name was different – he felt quite confused.
At playschool the kids' names were Kerry and Kim,
and Toby and Tina and Tessa and Tim.
Their names fitted perfectly onto their things,
their swirly-brush paintings and butterfly wings.

But Piggity's name would go all the way round,
and the name on his locker went right to the ground.

So when they had finally finished the book
and hung his red dressing-gown up on the hook,
Piggity-Wiggity Jiggity J
said to his dad, "I have something to say.
I'm cross, and I think you and Mum are to blame.
I'm afraid that you gave me the wrong kind of name.
It's long and it's lumpy, with far too much 'iggity'.
Please find me something not nearly so biggity!"

Dad turned and looked at his mutinous son,
whose inside-out jim-jams had buttons undone.
"I have a wee story to tell you," he said,
"but you need to be comfy, so hop into bed."

"Your mother and I had everything planned,
a family, a house, with a small piece of land.
The home and the section were easy to find
and soon we were thrilled to have four of each kind.

"But deep in our hearts, amidst fighting and kissing,
we knew there was one little pig that was missing.

"And then you were born to us, cherished and chosen,
one wintery night that was frosty and frozen.
You gurgled and chuckled and smiled as you sat,
in your fluffy new nappies and snug, woolly hat,
and we felt it would be a preposterous shame,
if we gave our small squealer a second-hand name.

"We wanted a name that had rhythm and style,
that would perk up your morning and brighten your smile.
A name that was dynamite, different and daring . . .
a name that epitomised kindness and caring,
a marvellous melody, music to hum,
a name that would pound like a beat on a drum!"

His voice got excited and slightly frenetic,
his flowery phrases became quite poetic.

"Ahem," he said suddenly, scratching his ear.
"It's just an old story I thought you should hear."
Then he pulled up the duvet and straightened it out,
and kissed his small son on the end of his snout.

As Piggity-Wiggity lay in his bed,
he basked in the glory of what had been said.

He whispered his name and he practised out loud,
and all down his spine he felt precious and proud.
His name was indeed very longity-long,
but deep down inside he felt strongity-strong.

His countenance glowed and his confidence grew;
his world was all sunshine because he now knew,
that Piggity-Wiggity Jiggity Jig . . .

was a smart sort of name
for a cool kind of pig.